DISNEY·PIXAR

MONSTERS, IN

MONSTERS GET SCARED OF THE DARK, TOO

By Melissa Lagonegro

Illustrated by Atelier Philippe Harchy

Random House 🏠 New York

ISBN: 978-0-7364-3056-2
randomhouse.com/kids
MANUFACTURED IN CHINA
10 9 8 7 6 5 4 3 2 1
Glow Art and Production: Red Bird Publishing Ltd., UK.

Mike and Sulley were going to have a fun night. They were monster-sitting Mike's nephew, Billy.

"Now, you be good," said Billy's mother as she waved good-bye.

"Don't worry, Mom, I will," replied Billy.

"Everything will be fine, Sis," said Mike proudly. "Sulley and I will take good care of the little guy."

And they did. The three monsters had a blast. They watched classic movies like *Night of the Living Kids* and *Gross Encounters of the Kid Kind* and ate lots of junk food.

They played Billy's favorite games . . .

listened to music . . .

and battled one another in tons of video games.

It got late, and that meant bedtime for Billy.
"It's time for some shut-eye," said Mike with a yawn.
"Lights out!"

But putting Billy to bed wasn't going to be that simple. Billy's mother had forgotten to tell her monster-sitters something important.

Billy was afraid of the dark!
"Aaaaaaahhhhh!" screamed Billy after Mike and
Sulley closed his bedroom door. "UNCLE MIIIIKE!"

"Wh-wh-what is it?" shouted Mike as he and Sulley ran
back into the room.
"There's a k-kid hiding in the c-closet . . . ," stuttered
Billy. "It wants to g-get me!"

Mike and Sulley searched the room.
"No kids in the closet," said Mike.
"All clear under the bed," announced Sulley.

But Billy was still scared. Sulley and Mike needed a plan.
"I've got it!" exclaimed Mike. "The scrapbook!"
"You're a genius, Mikey!" declared Sulley.

The monster-sitters hopped onto the bed next to Billy, and they all looked through Mike and Sulley's scrapbook. It was filled with pictures of monsters with kids, laugh reports, and Boo's drawings.

"See, Billy?" said Mike. "Human kids aren't dangerous, and they love to have fun, just like you."

"And they help!" added Sulley. "Their laughter powers our city!"

NO MORE ENERGY CRISIS
SCREAMS TURN TO LAUGHS

Now monsters can make kids laugh. Kids' laughter is more powerful than their screams.

"You know, Billy, sometimes human kids get scared of *us*," said Mike. "But once they see that we're funny and friendly, they realize there's no reason to be scared of monsters."

"This scrapbook shows that there's no reason for you to be scared of human kids," added Sulley. "But just in case you get scared again, we'll leave it here. You can look through it to make yourself feel better."

Billy fell fast asleep as his uncle
watched from the doorway.

"Another job well done, Mike,"
said Sulley.

"We're still the best team in the biz,"
replied Mike.